How
THINDER
WOMAN
MET THE
GARDEN

A Picture Book of Botanical Consciousness

Forest Bae

Illustrated by
Forest Bae & Felice Bedford

TIVOLI PRESS
USA . ITALY

Published by Tivoli Press
USA
Philadelphia, Pennsylvania
Manufactured in the United States of America

ISBN: 979-8-9886102-9-8
Library of Congress Control Number: forthcoming

The characters and events depicted are fictional
and not intended to represent actual occurrences,
circumstances or persons.

No plants were harmed in the creation of this
work. The author wishes to thank Anette
Strawberry for *"strawberry fingers forever"* and
Sue Giraffe for continued encouragement.

For the Garden Whisperer.

<u>Ground</u>

There's a door.
It's green.
Come in.
--S.W.

"Yes, it IS
a great
idea-but
I can't
find us
a garden
feeling
like this.
Doggone it!"

Somewhere, the garden was out there, unearthing its own drama.

"Look at me!"
said the Shasta daisy.

"Show off!!"
teased the rosebud sapling.

"Grandma, will I still hear her
when I grow tall like you?"

Grandma Rosalee thought and thought.

"

"My dearest seedling,
When your thick trunk grows tall
And your heart leaves shrink small
Yes, you will still hear her call—
But by then you'll be above it all."

Blue Flax is the
mellow man of the meadow.

Is he sleeping again?
Does he dream?

Still?

They're here!
Let's watch if the
Midday Sun Visitors
wake Floyd up!

(Yes, he dreams)

He's up.

Now the Johnny Jump Ups
are up
...and up...Watch out!

While there is just one or two,
they sure spring out

at You.

But we have so many...

...mock strawberries this year

Come on Felix! Just use
those windmill-like arms you've
got to swat them away!" I feel so
bad for the fleabane. He just
arrived from Philly and the dancing
black cloud won't stop bugging the
new plant in town.

"Ok—Who sneezed near the sow?"

The air becomes thick with thistle
seed.
Dreamy for some, nightmare for
others.

And when the
Mightiest Wind visits,
the daisies have
an especially hard time.

Ha Ha! Look at me!
♫ *I'm a Shasta daze-eee!* ♫
Ha Ha Ha!

"Not funny," protested Rosalee's grandson, the rosebud sapling.

"Look! He wiped out Judy's whole family. He's coming! I'm afraid!"

WORSE THAN WIND

"Don't worry. We can fight back
with our chemical teeth."

But She Who Scratches is our friend.

She protects us.

"You can come scratch here
anytime, Foxy Lady."

"How should we fill the bare patch left by He Who Hops and Harms?"

"Ok, Let's get moving on this, Plants!

Never give a coreopsis a clipboard.

They're so bold!

"Give 'em a break. They have a tough time with those yellow missiles all day."

He looks
heavy!

Sigh

Maybe the new one will fill the
bare patch and deal with the
cruel white snake root, too.

Strangle. Sting. Spread.
Even a dumb bunny learns
not to get too close to me.

Above Ground

There's a door.
It's pink.
Come up.
--S.W.

Meanwhile, a few feet higher than
us,
the human tried everything to get
well.
She even visited distant worlds.

--S.W.

You should eat

MORE

You should eat
LESS

You
need
more
sun

Have
you
tried
desert
therapy
?

(The blank stare)

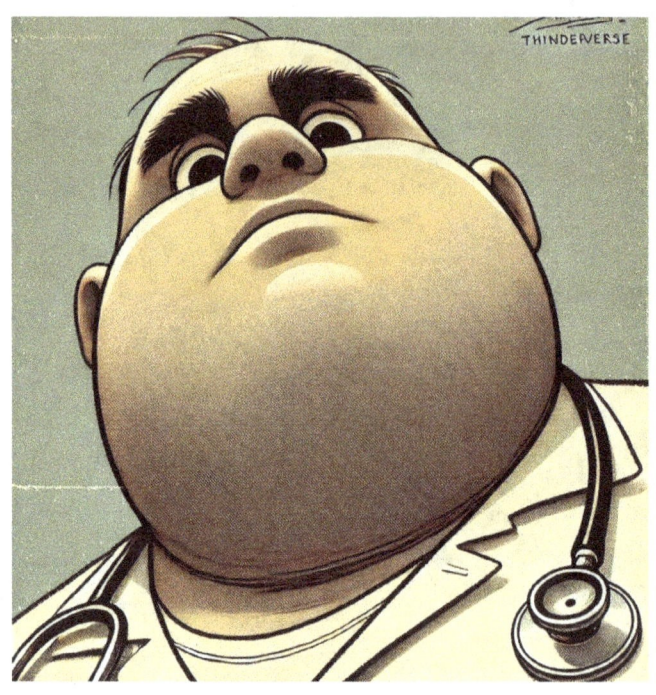

And she visited distant **times!**

Phleboto

Jan. 1, 2075

but always returned,
no wiser.

"Fern! Over here. It's Steph. The
real estate agent?
I have a house to show you."

"Many stairs. No garden."

"Train noise. No garden."

"Um, no"

"Seriously
?"

"This is it!"

"Who is she?"

"She smells like ozone."

"Friend or foe?"

"Fox or rabbit?"

"I like her."

"'Ha Ha Ha'"

"Boing!"

"She's fills the bare patch nicely."

"I vote to pick her."

"Let's keep her."

"Come meet your neighbors before
I head back to the office."

"Yup, we have men and boys
here—just not as many."

"And here's my son, Bean Sprout. He grows the hybrid-human vegetables, you know, the strawberry fingers? And nosey pumpkins and ears of corn that hear—look closely.

♫ *Strawberry fingers forever* ♫ & all the collieflowers, of course."

I
can let
her see
the
garden
now.
--S.W.

Who am I?
You can call me Sweet William.
Everyone does.
I've been around. Narrating a little.

We call our garden Redgrove.
There's a different perspective in
If You Like Animals
Better Than People.
Yes, the legendary Sprout
is still here.

Come stay with us?

"Nice to meet you, too.
What's that about collecting the
microbiota in the earth
to help me?"

Hmmm

Wow! this...this...*Thinder Woman*
even tamed the white snake root!
I knew we picked well.

Better Times

Welcome to the Thinderverse

The End

# Back Ground

Once upon a time...

flowers lost their garden green
when they bud,

then were befriended by
the Midday Sun Visitors

and had an awkward adolescence,

but like all flowers in the garden,
they found a way to reseed
themselves,

and so, there cane to be many
collieflowers
in the Thinderverse.

Also by the Author

All Cab Drivers Look Alike (Science)

Who's Lucky Here Anyway?

Who is Lucky? (bilingual)

If You Like Animals Better than People

Mystery by the Maple

Day Trading for Presents (Finance)

The Names of Gnomes (with Rosie Oliver)